T0381142

LIFE
IS BEAUTIFUL
PART -2

MANISH GURUNG

AuthorHouse™ UK
1663 Liberty Drive
Bloomington, IN 47403 USA
www.authorhouse.co.uk
UK TFN: 0800 0148641 (Toll Free inside the UK)
UK Local: 02036 956322 (+44 20 3695 6322 from outside the UK)

Because of the dynamic nature of the Internet, any web addresses or links contained in this book may have changed since publication and may no longer be valid. The views expressed in this work are solely those of the author and do not necessarily reflect the views of the publisher, and the publisher hereby disclaims any responsibility for them.

This book is printed on acid-free paper.

ISBN: 979-8-8230-8278-5 (sc)
ISBN: 979-8-8230-8279-2 (hc)
ISBN: 979-8-8230-8280-8 (e)

Library of Congress Control Number: 2022046892

Print information available on the last page.

Published by AuthorHouse 06/12/2023

author HOUSE®

Contents

Dedication..v

Acknowledgements... vi

About the Author.. vii

Author's Note viii

Introduction..ix

The Death.. 1

The New Born.. 7

The Living.. 15

The Twinkle Star.. 21

The Peaceful Sunset.. 37

Receiving As It Comes.. 45

Forgiving.. 51

Dedication

This book is dedicated to all those common people who are alive after coming out of depression. This books tells them that it's ok to not have a car, it's ok you're not successful at work or relationships. It's ok to make mistakes, it's ok to be sad, it's ok to be low sometimes and it's ok to cry alone.

It's ok for you to feel fresh air, sunlight and life's beauty first hand. You just need to be unapologetically yourself!

Acknowledgements

I would like to express my deepest gratitude,

To my Idol, my parents,

My thoughts wouldn't have turn into a book without my beloved parents who stood steadfast with faith, dealt with hardships just to educate me.

To my brother, his wife and their children for all the love and support they gave me. My little sister Vidhya.

To my son.

To my dearest friend Rebecca who encouraged me timely to work on my book and all other friends who were a part of my life's journey... Chanchal, Vilma, Alina Coasta, Reka, Amit J., Sabina, Parvaiz, Dorina, Cosmina, Valentina, Maria V, Allan, Akira, Chris, Samir Alena, Simone, Asma, Asha and many others.

Thank you all!

About the Author

Manish Gurung has been working in the hospitality industry for the last 23 years. He has extensive experience in managing hotels, specifically in Room division and Revenue Management.

His early education was a bachelor's degree in hotel management, but he also has knowledge in several other areas, such as personal management, human resources, business management, psychology, motivation and many more.

He has worked with several luxurious properties and has a vast experience in hotel management and people management.

His idol and inspiration in writing this book are his parents, his brother and his family, and most importantly, his lovely son.

Life is Beautiful is the author's first book. Other than writing, the author has a deep interest in travelling, drawing, music and dancing.

Author's Note

This book is a work of fiction, but it is based on some real-life experiences. The names of persons, institutions and a few other details have been changed to protect the identities of all mentioned herein.

The book is not at all about bipolar disorder. It is a story of courage, determination and growing up. It's also about how life can take a totally different path from what you have planned. In the world at large, mental health issues have now elevated to a point where they have acquired the status of becoming 'celebrity disorder' with several well-known people coming out and admitting they have those, such as Mel Gibson and Ozzy Osbourne, to name a few.

This book shows the mental instability that affects moods, energy levels, attitudes and the ability to perform everyday tasks. It shows how mental health begins deteriorating in childhood, leads on to adolescence and even seeps into early adulthood. It can be very creepy, sometimes affecting one's performance at a job or in academia. It has the potential to damage relationships. During low periods, people experiencing any form of mental disorder feel worthlessness, empty, and exhausted and often lose interest in living their lives. This is the reason many people affected by mental health issues think of death and attempting suicide quite often.

Life is Beautiful lets the reader take a peek into the life of a man called Bruce, who faced several downfalls in his life, but he learns to cope with them.

There is a common perception that, perhaps, coping entails getting back into the world and its struggles and becoming immaculately successful. However, that is quite contrary to reality. In real life, even if one is able to climb out of depression, even when they carry grief with them and maintain a mindset of not falling back into depression, their life can also be successful.

Introduction

Life is valued by those...who have seen death.

The Death

"Death is the mother of beauty. Only the perishable can be beautiful, which is why we are unmoved by artificial flowers."

It was an early summer evening. I could feel the slight chill in the air - a little foggy and wet air settled about at Sundown. A half-empty bottle of Single Malt Whiskey lay on the floor near the bathtub in the room of a 4-star hotel.

I could see the lights on the ceiling fading away as my eyes slowly moved with the water waves on their brims. There was absolute silence. There was no sound, not even that of breathing and the lights around me were fading into darkness. Soon there was nothing but blackness, no sound, no light, no thoughts, no heartbeats...

Suddenly, my body jerked out from the bathtub, fell back into it for a moment as I went underwater, choked for breath then pulled myself up again. I took a deep breath, stood up, dried myself up, went over to my bed and just crashed.

Morning came along quite quickly. I got up with my head hurting like hell. It took a few minutes to understand where I was. For a moment, I thought perhaps I had tried to do something stupid.

Was it a suicide??!!!

I had a heavy hangover. My head was hurting as if it had been banging against the wall all night. I still managed to drag my body out of bed and went for breakfast at the hotel restaurant around 9 am. I was greeted very politely by the hotel staff. The hostess was slim and well-dressed in a uniform, and her hair was tied in a high ponytail. She had a nice smile on her face. The dark blue uniform suited her height perfectly.

Hostess: *Very good morning, Mr Bruce, we have a table reserved for you!*

Bruce: *Oh, thank you.*

Hostess: *We have a buffet, kindly help yourself, and if you need anything, we are happy to assist.*

Bruce: *I am fine, thank you.*

I took a toast and fried egg, sunny side up, with some bacon. The waitress poured me black coffee, which I needed the most.

After a while, a gentleman approached me. He was gentle, tall and had a trimmed beard like mine. He wore a dark grey suit. It was not uniform. It could be his personal suit, but he had a company badge pinned to his chest.

Good morning, Mr Bruce, how is your stay going?

Bruce: *Great, thank you.*

My name is... (I can't remember his name as I was in a hangover). I am the Duty Manager here.

Bruce: *Nice to meet you.*

Duty Manager: *Are you feeling better now?*

I felt odd about people being so kind to me!

Bruce: *Yes, I just have a slight headache. Might have had an extra drink. Was I ok? (I don't know why I asked that question?)*

Duty Manager: *Absolutely, sir, I understand an occasion for drinks, however, I would just like to bring to your notice that we have a non-smoking hotel, and we would request you to use our designated smoking area just outside the lobby. Also, we would like to let you know that the cops visited you on your call to them and left a message to call them if anything was required.*

Bruce: *I am so sorry for all the mess.*

Duty Manager: *Not at all, sir. Just be careful and enjoy breakfast.*

My head was now exploding! What had I done?!

I probably smoked in the room, the fire alarm must have gone off, the staff would have gathered, and even cops were there. I probably made too many calls to emergency services!

I left my breakfast halfway, gulped down my coffee and checked out from the hotel immediately. My head was coming to somewhat by now, and my toothache was adding to the pain. I have had this toothache for the last few days. I went to the shop and got two miniature whiskeys, and emptied them. I sat on the bench near the wine shop. My breathing was still heavy, and I could see the vape of my hot breath into the air. It was 10 am and a bit cold outside. It was 12°C that morning. It took me a few minutes to calm down till my breathing became normal. I went straight home.

"Alcohol is not the answer to all questions...but it helps to forget the question!!"

Life is difficult. It might give you a few things. You might even be happy for a while as you achieve whatever goals you set to achieve: a college degree, a job, a nice house, and maybe even marriage to your dream partner. Life keeps you busy with mundane things, and you chug along, happy to receive that promotion, happy to move into a bigger house, drive a better car, and earn more money.

Eventually, life comes to collect. It takes away everything that means a lot to you. It takes away your youth, and if you are not careful, your health and your peace of mind too. In the course of your life, you eventually lose your grandparents and then your parents. Perhaps you even lose a spouse or a child.

How, then, do you go on? What meaning can you derive from it all? How do you overcome the debilitating grief of losing all you hold dear?

The rest of my next few days went by in bare consciousness in drinking. I went to the dentist as well, but I don't remember when I called them and booked the appointment.

There was a call one morning.

Caller: *Good morning, Mr Bruce. I am calling from the dental care clinic. Just calling to confirm your appointment. You are running late for your appointment at 10 am.*

I realised I must have made the booking.

Bruce: *Oh, yes, got some emergency. Can I postpone to another time, please? (Shit!)*

Caller: *Let me check...will 13:00 hrs be fine?*

Bruce: *Yes, perfect.*

I jumped out of my bed, got a bit sober, washed and reached the dental clinic.

The doctor became available quickly, and the examination began.

Doctor: *You need a small surgery.*

Bruce: *Okay, when?*

Doctor: *Next week, but you need to take medicines until then.*

Bruce: *Okay.*

Doctor: *One tablet a day only. It's a very strong medicine. But not a single drop of alcohol with the tablets. (The doctor could tell as my mouth was stinking with alcohol.)*

Bruce: *Okay, of course not. I had a get-together party yesterday.*

Doctor: *Great, see you next week!*

Bruce: *Sure, thank you, doctor.*

A few days went by as a drunk, and I don't really remember anything. It was like,

NO TRANSMISSION ON TV

The next thing I remember straight was that I was sitting on my bed with my tablets. I felt it was time to sleep... I did not see the time, but it was certainly dark outside. I probably hadn't slept properly for days, or I don't remember what sleep was.

Today, I am prepared to sleep as if I have nothing to do the next day. No work, no cooking, no washing, no shopping, no news, nothing on my mind.

I am feeling free... From what? I don't know...but my head is feeling lighter today.

It was the first time I made my bed before going to sleep. The sheets were neatly tucked in the sides. I adjusted my pillows. I use two pillows always. My duvet was ready to slip into. I was in my pyjamas already.

I popped in all four tablets with whisky. I could hear the doctor's words softly in the background of not having the tablets with drinks as it was very, very dangerous.

I slipped under the quilt and slept like a baby.

I was happy to sleep, I don't know why?

I knew what I was doing, I was in my complete senses.

I just decided to die in my sleep.

> **When death starts looking more beautiful than life, then you
> know life can't adorn you any more with scars**

The New Born

If you keep one hand on your past and one hand
on your future, you'll never have either.

To embrace tomorrow, you must let go of yesterday.

Sunrays were hitting me in my eyes through the window the next morning. I was staring at the ceiling, wondering if it was my room I had awoken in. Where was I? Was it morning or afternoon...? Well, first, I understood who I was and what I was doing here. Then came other things...What year it was? What age was I? Who were my parents...etc.? All questions flashed into my head in a fraction of a second, and I realised what the present scenario of my life was. Still laying on the bed, I came to know that I had tried to commit suicide. I tried moving my head, my hands, and my legs and tried to get up. I sat on my bed and realised that...**I was alive...But WHY?**

To cure the headache, for the first time in my life, I made coffee instead of whiskey. I brushed my teeth, dressed up and walked out, not knowing where I was going. I just walked about and saw what I could not see in my very drunk days.

I saw a broken down car near my house and realised it had been there for ages...but I had only seen it today. It was an old classic Chevrolet in light pink colour. I saw many things around me which were there, but I had never noticed them. I went outside for window shopping. I did not buy anything, but it was a nice feeling to watch everything that was there in the shops. Things only this generation can enjoy. It has been years since I have been to shopping this way.

My mind felt like it was blank and empty. It felt like everything was gone, or it didn't affect me anymore or something along those lines. I did not understand the feelings in my head, or perhaps there were no feelings.

All others... society, money, prestige, status, the power I had nothing left. And I did not want it. I had lost everything for these things but not anymore.

I was f*ed up, but why others I cared about had to go to hell with me and suffer like me? Why do I have to? And **NOW** I don't want to die...I realised life is something to live... **But for what?**

My parents used to cry when they were talking to me. My brother and his wife were worried for me. Why?? I had given them nothing but trouble and pain so far. It was not that I had done it on purpose, but my condition had dragged us all to hell and back. I had decided then that I would make them proud one day. I didn't know how I would do it. I didn't have an executable action plan, but I wanted it more than anything else in the world.

I started yoga and gym, and I booked a few consultations with a psychiatrist as well.

Psychiatrist: *Hi Bruce, what's up?*

Bruce: *Doctor, I cannot concentrate! I write my schedule on papers minute-by-minute, what time to sleep, eat, brush, cook, wash, drink, and smoke...even breathe.*

Psychiatrist: *Well, I do that, but I still forget things. That's normal. How long do you do yoga?*

Bruce: *One hour, then I cannot do it anymore.*

Psychiatrist: *Leave yoga.*

Bruce: *What? What do you mean? Yoga is good!*

Psychiatrist: *Of course, it is the best, but if you're stressed by doing it...don't do it... Bruce, just remember you must do everything you can to reduce stress, and if it comes to that, anything you do that gets you stressed while doing it...just don't do it... simple.*

And he was right...Don't force yourself to get de-stressed...you will feel more stressed.

My work with the psychiatrist did more than what I had hoped for. It gave me the direction I had been missing for a very long time. It gave me some form of perspective I had lost to the drinking. I began to implement the advice I had gotten from the psychiatrist. I started my day with just ten minutes of yoga, but I did more gym as it did not stress me.

I also started spending more time with my son. He is ten years old now. I have a complicated relationship with my son. We are often not as close as we'd like to be, but I try my best to be the father he expects me to be.

I try to take him out from time to time, but nothing is the same as before. Today's generation is more interested in spending time on Roblox instead of indulging in physical activities. Surprisingly, I was also able to reduce my drinking habit. Now I drank only in the evenings and on the weekends.

Spending more time with my son brought me many realisations. Reduced drinking cleared my head, and I was able to see my son more clearly than before. I noticed his phone had an alarm that went off at 7:30 am every day so he could get up for school. He kept his shoelaces tied up permanently so he did not have to tie them up daily. Among other things, he never asked me unnecessary questions. He never wanted to know why I lived separately. He had shown me more maturity than most kids his age. He didn't deserve this. He deserved a normal life with a father he could be proud of. He is not supposed to bear the burden he does.

Other kids his age were carefree and livelier than my son. They loved and enjoyed life to the fullest while my son carried the weight of the world on his shoulders. I felt he ought to live his life as per his age and enjoy the fun activities that come with his age. He should enjoy little things like being woken up every day for school, looking forward to going to play with his friends, to argue with friends over trifles, to shout and scream with joy at the top of his lungs, to laugh his heart out, to love himself and those around him to the fullest but he did not have that privilege. My son lived with his mom after my ex-wife and I got divorced after 10 years of our marriage.

Although the decision to part ways was mutual between my wife and me, I took the toll of the decision. My family didn't know that for a very long time. I managed to keep quiet about how I was truly feeling after the divorce but it didn't do me any favours. I indulged in a really bad drinking habit that drowned me in sorrow and depression. In front of my parents, I behaved very differently.

I began pretending that I was happy and fine. I made my parents believe that I had gotten out of depression. For a very long time, I couldn't stand the helpless expression on their faces. They gave me pleading looks, and they panicked when they saw me in pain. All of their feelings were too much for me to bear. I couldn't bear the depth of their love. They loved me unconditionally, no matter what state of mind I was in. No matter how broken I was, they were always there for me. God bless my parents, I knew they didn't deserve this. I had had enough. I could not face them anymore. I didn't want them to be a part of any of this. I had given them enough pain in the last few years when I had massive problems in my married life.

I learned a lot from my personal failures in life and one of the major lessons I learned was that no matter how different our parents' outlook towards life is from ours, the one thing we often overlook is that they are on our side. Our parents always try and do what is best for us. Sometimes, we feel that our parents' actions restrict us, but what they do is only beneficial for us.

When we are kids, they only restrict us where our safety is concerned. When they think something endangers us, they tell us not to do those things. They ask us not to play with matches. They ask us not to touch electrical wires. They ask us not to go to the edge of the terrace. They train us not to cross the road without looking. They repeat these instructions to us so many times that it becomes ingrained in us and our behaviour to the point that these instructions become rules that we follow on a daily basis.

We never question these rules because the implications of breaking them are obvious always. But, sometimes, the implications are not so obvious. We doubt them, then. I think it is okay to doubt them. In fact, it is important to question them. That is the only way we grow and the only way we become adults - by weighing our opinions, which are usually heavily against theirs and then taking a decision based on facts that are evident to us. Sometimes we hide these facts.

All is good as long as we do not get into trouble and are able to manage things on our own. But nothing's in our control. Things go horribly wrong, and then we do not know what to do. Then we turn to our parents. When we do turn to them, our parents don't care whether we followed the rules or not, they are always there for us. They do the best they can in the given circumstances. They may scold us, reprimand us, and shout at us, but mostly they take care of us.

If you have a set of parents who are in your corner, no matter what, it is a massive strength. Parents can be your wings when yours are broken and you need a little help to fly.

With care, love and understanding, anything can heal. Anything.

I pretended so well though. My parents were elated that everything was finally going well. They were relieved that the days of psychiatric imbalance were far behind. I let them believe it, not wanting to burst their bubble. But I was exactly where I had been when I started out with my depression. Our defeats are magnified in our own heads because we focus on what we have lost rather than on what we actually have. We lose perspective of how blessed we are. If we have the love of our parents, if we have people who care for us, if we have a hot meal on the table, then we are blessed. When I realised how important it was to have parents, I decided to be there for my son. I started spending time with my son without any other reason or thoughts in mind. I was feeling free as if I was not scared of anything since I had just met death a few days back!

When it comes to the big things in life, it is important to speak the truth, no matter how hard it is or how unpleasant it is. When we do not speak the truth about the big things, then we end up hurting ourselves.

Our life makes up of a lot of small things and big things. We need to be wise enough to make a distinction between what is a small thing and what is a big thing. Sometimes, a small thing to us is a big thing to others. At other times, a big thing to us is a small thing to others. If we have people in our lives who treat and understand how big our small things to us are, then we are fortunate. I think when people are on the same wavelength, they completely get each other. It doesn't matter how many big or small things you deal with as long as you have each other. You know that the other person will be there for you - to see you through the big and small things in life and that you will be there for them too. It is rare, but if you have it, you are blessed. If you have it, you are the richest person on Earth.

The headspace I had landed into in my life took me to the place where people didn't matter anymore. I just made people happy, whoever was in the flow. Time also didn't matter neither did status, prestige, appearance, clothes or anything else. I even deleted Facebook and Instagram. What did I have to post about anyway?

I started living a simple life. I ate simple, thought simple and acted simple. I let my parents believe that everything was fine when in reality, nothing was. I was surprised I could pretend so well to show my parents that things were great and that I was happy. While in reality, I was dying inside, yet I concealed it so well.

It was as if I was living a double life. There was one life that I showed to my parents, and then there was a life that I was actually living, one where I was never happy.

On my off days, I did some work then I pulled out the books. I felt so free that I couldn't find things to consume my time, but I still couldn't sleep at night. Sleep was elusive. However tightly I shut my eyes, it just wouldn't come. It had been like this for the past many nights. I was now tired of trying. Instead of praying for sleep, I decided I would read.

Ironically, I enjoyed reading a book about sleep disorders that I had bought to cure my sleeping disorder. I learnt that lack of sleep could slow down the cognitive process, making us testy, irritable and short-tempered. It can cause a lack of alertness. It impaired attention, concentration and focus. It also caused several health problems like heart disease, heart attack and even diabetes. A lack of sleep creates resistance to insulin in the human body. While reading this book, I felt astonished. It made me sit up and take notice. I continued to read on, finishing the book in a few hours.

Even a single night's lack of sleep sets us up to react more strongly and impulsively to negative situations. If we continue to operate on chronic sleep debt, we fall prey to heightened emotional reactivity. I learnt that sleep deprivation increased the activity in the amygdala, which was a part of the brain that controls our immediate emotional reactions. If we sleep less, the amygdala goes into overdrive and hampers communication with the pre-frontal cortex, the part of the brain that handles a lot of complex tasks and impulsiveness.

Once I read that, I started putting time into exercise, studying, watching the news and experiencing nature. I thought all of this activity would help me feel tired and I would be able to get some good sleep. Reading became my saviour. Whenever I felt like reading I read some good novels like, 'The Monk Who Sold His Ferrari' by Robin Sharma, 'The Courage To Be Disliked' by Fumitake Koga and Ichiro Kishimi, Half Girlfriend by Chetan Bhagat, etc. I engaged myself in reading and enjoying short studies about exercising, mental health, entrepreneurship, consciousness, managing business and managing people, self-motivation, personal branding and several others. I also read many books on the science of nutrition and healthy eating. I also achieved the Security Industry Authority (SIA) license in private security services. I also became a First Aider. Through reading and motivating myself, I managed to do a lot of things I hadn't been able to do ever before and yet I learned.

Life is a great teacher. It gives you exams but doesn't tell you the syllabus. It is up to us to set our own lessons. Reading made me feel better. It helped me cope with shame and pain.

For a while, I felt as if reading had done the job for me. It had healed me. I thought I had dealt with all the bad things. I felt as if the love and support I was getting from my family was bringing me back to the normal I had missed for a very long time. I felt so grateful for their love and support. It all allowed me to push back the memories a little further. But I didn't know I wasn't healing as well as I thought I was.

I battled with myself on a daily basis. If only anyone knew how difficult it was. If only anyone knew how I was filled with self-doubt, how I lay awake each night worrying too much and sleeping too little. Both always came back to my room, the shame and the humiliation. I learnt to reign in my sadness and keep it inside me. I began choosing carefully who I let in and who I needed to leave outside. I decided I wouldn't give my mind space to everyone.

I will live, live for my parents, my family, and my son and enjoy the beauty of all things around me.

When it hurts, observe. Life is trying to teach you something

The Living

I am in competition with no one. I have no desire to play the game of being better with anyone. I am simply trying to be better than the person I was yesterday.

After the incident (let's call my suicide attempt an accident), my life changed completely. I shut down socially and I kept my profile very low. I began working as a mid-manager working for a multinational company in different shifts. My daily routine became gym, work, alcohol, food, TV and sleep. I wasn't very well-known in the office circle as well. I didn't want to be known by anyone. The fewer people knew me the better it was. What would I share with them anyway? That my life was in shambles? My marriage didn't exist? My son was falling into the same trap of depression I was going through? And that I was barely keeping it together? Nope, not a great conversation over lunch.

I planned my weekends well too. As my weekends were off days, I would bring my son over to stay with me. My weekends began compensating for my bland weekdays.

I would cook for my son or order his favourite food. We sometimes went for a movie or in the park or shopping or I would just let him play around.

I do have one friend, CK. I stay with him and his family. They are very dear to me and theirs is my second home besides my parents'. They have been exceptionally kind to me and have accepted me as a family. Their kids call me uncle. My son loves to hang out with them as well and enjoys playing with their kids.

Long before 'the incident', I had completed multiple degrees in the field of Management and diplomas in Business Administration, HRD, Personal Management, Counselling Psychology and Stress Management. I was an operations manager at the last company I was working at before the incident. I owned a bungalow with a garden, and a car and remember living my life and working for money, status, and pride. I had friends connected in high places and I was considered a wise guy, a made man (just like those in gangster movies). Money was nothing, I played with status. I was known down 10 blocks.

Back then I didn't know but I was driving myself deeper into the ground. It was as if I had some kind of death wish. Nothing ever satisfied me. Eventually, my marriage failed, I no longer spoke with my parents much, and though I had every material possession anyone could want, I did not find what I was looking for. It had a toll on me emotionally, physically and spiritually. At thirty-five years of age, I looked as if I was in my late fifties. My face was a mass of wrinkles, a less than a glorious tribute to my "take-no-prisoners" approach to life in general and the tremendous stress of my out-of-balance lifestyle in particular including but not limited to the late-night dinners in expensive restaurants, smoking thick cigars and drinking cognac after cognac, all of which had left me embarrassingly overweight. I constantly complained that I was sick and tired of being sick and tired. I had lost my sense of humour and I never seemed to laugh anymore.

My life took a 360-degree turn after 'the accident'. The first thing I did was change the city I lived in. I could use a little bit of new and time away from the same old same old. My first job after 'the incident' was too short-lived. I spent a lot of time understanding the new city. I also felt depressed all the time. My depression and unfamiliarity with the city caused me to lose my first job quite quickly. My second job was nice and I felt I fit into it a little bit. I met a few interesting people at my second job.

At the second job, AC was my first colleague whom I respect a lot and who is still in touch with me. She is a wonderful woman who knows a bit about my present life. She has daughters who accompany her and she is enjoying seeing them grow up into adults. I visited her last year. We still share messages once in a while. My second job ended in a year because the company I was working for closed down for a year and I was transferred to a sister company to provide assistance. The time I stayed at the sister concern was very joyful and all my colleagues were very good. When I was leaving back to my old company, they saw me off with hugs and told me they would miss me. I made several new friends there. PY was my close colleague and we still remain a good friend. He is now settled in a director's position and has a lovely family. I and PY were the first to join the company.

Other than PY, AK & CB were my first field colleagues on the shift and we shared all of our rough and happy moments during our work tenure.

Since the company we were working for had only just started, we had to struggle for every little thing. But we were very efficient people, especially VALI who was the first gentle and mature lady I had met long after post-incident. She was a lovely lady. She has her own events company now and she is as gorgeous as always. Another one of my colleagues was DN who was a bit tomboyish but a very kind and fun-loving lady. But she had a habit of getting pissed off pretty soon.

Another interesting colleague I had was Cos who was a sweet little girl and we both shared a few little laughs between us. She is in her home country now and happily married. Ale was another nice lady that was working with me. She had a baby when she still was with the company. The women at my company were all unique and had their own personalities. MV was a tough lady. She was very active, a young old NINJA of my age, jumping around all the time, getting things done. She is still in touch with me. She lives in her country now enjoying the countryside but she is still as rough as the old days. And then there was SW, my boss, who was always too serious and into work but I don't know how we used to work and have so much fun and comedy. I remember her bursting into laughter when we talked.

Bruce: *The old man has come to clean the carpet and I don't know whether the man is shaking more or the machine.*

SW: *HAHAHAHA (she burst into laughter)*

While working with her, we had a lot of fun, although she was only there for a short period of time. We are still friends and I still call her my BOSS! She is the top Executive Director of a multinational company. Work is where you can find her always, as usual.

While work meant a lot to me, so did my son and I made sure to give him as much time as possible. When he stayed with me, he had my undivided attention. Whenever my son stayed at his mom's place, I invested some of my time into the office and then some of it into travelling to work. I made a habit of getting to the office, two hours earlier than needed. I used to take the longest route so I could watch everything on the way. When I reached the office, I would freshen up and then watch the news or message a few people just to say hello. Then I would have some coffee with a few cigarettes. When the rest of the staff came, I always shared a conversation such as this with them.

Staff: *Hey Bruce! You starting or finishing? (Hahaha!) Why are you so early??*

Bruce: *I love my job! (Hahaha!)*

Staff: *You are crazy man...anyways, enjoy your day!*

Bruce: *Thanks, same shit different day!*

The company I was working for became my second home, so much so that I stayed there for the longest time. Everyone left the company and continued their career or life. I was still there with the new people joining and leaving. But I had a nice time with the people I mentioned above. Other than that, I hated everyone.

The only routine I had was being on the job and then coming back home. I just wanted to be alone. I had no sense of social networking, gatherings or friends in particular. I just met people when I met them at work or in passing but I made sure whoever I met, I made them smile. I didn't have the ambition or the eagerness to grow into my career or to build money or status. I was just passing my life without needing anything special. Many of my colleagues offered me jobs with better prospects but I turned everyone down. How would I explain to them that I was working just to pay my bills and I didn't need more. Time had flown since 'the accident'. My life had changed to just being one where I was living to live. My son was a teenager now and he had his own life. He had moved on from the sorrows of the past and I was hoping to do the same.

Living a life like this made me realise a lot of things about life. We often worry too much about what others will think of us and how they will behave. We also ponder over the choices others make without understanding that we are not responsible for the choices others make.

We always forget that we are not responsible for other people's actions. Others' actions are the choices they make. Can we control how others behave? That is the question we must ask ourselves every day. You cannot control how anyone behaves towards you. You should not have to carry the blame for anyone's behaviour. You cannot blame yourself by assuming that it was something you did that made them act in a certain way. They are free to make their own choices. We do not control others. We only control our own minds. We should do everything we can to keep our minds in check.

We often fall prey to the fact that someone misbehaves with us or hurts us but we beat ourselves for it. We must realise, we do not have any control over other people's choices. Yet we beat ourselves over it. I suggest differently. Face the grief. Acknowledge it. Accept that it exists. Cry if you must, but limit it to ten minutes or maybe twenty. After that, do things that heal your soul. Find out what satisfies you on a deeper level or anything that you forgot in your minutiae.

During this time period, I managed to make things stable with my job, I also visited some places. My son and I went to Scotland for three days. I travelled alone to Spain for a few days randomly. I visited many good places with my son. We watched movies together, went to gaming arcades and went shopping. The rest of my time was work-home, home-work.

At present, my only wish is to look for an old age home and retire for the future. I also plan to donate my organs when I die. That's how I have decided to live the rest of my life.

It has now been seven years since I have begun living a simple life and sharing smiles with everyone I meet. I have kept all the grief within me. Nights are the only time that I keep for myself. No one I have met in the last seven years has become so close to me, who I can share my grief with. In fact, now I don't want anyone to share my life or grief with. I was actually doing quite well living alone. I was living a simple life, eating simple, and thinking simple.

I have been in the same company for the last five years. It is in the same building as before, and it has the same colour. For all these past years, people joined the company and left. There are very few colleagues of mine who have stayed in touch with me for a few years but they are also slowly fading away. I was never eager to change my company as I was not bothered about anything. My life was all about home, work, my son and the people I met for a few months and they keep changing.

...until there, once saw a shooting star! Except it was in the daytime...

The Twinkle Star

Sometimes, we are like stars...

We fall to make someone's wish come true!

The smile that makes me alive! The star that twinkles into my eyes!!

The walk was my first after seven years, and it felt like I was gliding with nature. She is a creature of nature with hairs like the autumn breeze and eyes like deep oceans but twinkling and innocent. Her smile has a double curve, and it comes straight from the heart. She normally doesn't always smile from the heart. After years, I had come out like this. I felt fresh. The company I had was so warm and gentle, as if nature had taken ample time to create her. I was speaking to her as if I had been talking to her and known her for years! To date, whenever I close my eyes, I can see her clearly and feel her presence all the time. Even now, the air around me feels like a sweater of hers, giving me warmth.

She was working with me in the same office, and she was young, but she had the maturity of listening and understanding, and she was well aware of life. It was as if she had a very close encounter with life in the past. We hardly met face-to-face or talked, but we always acknowledged each other. Slowly, we began talking about office politics, and the conversations went on too long and even moved to messages over the phone.

She was a well-educated young lady, but she still had a bit of old-school touch and values she always upheld. She was very gentle, calm and an exceptionally good listener. She always talks sense, almost all of the time. She and I could understand each other without even completing full sentences. I don't know why but the energy around our individual bodies blended well; when we were around, we didn't feel uneasy.

I was always known to be a ghost. No one knew much about me. They knew only what I wanted them to know. I like to study people, and people like to talk to me. But this was the first time in my life when I talked all about myself. Rebecca and I spoke a lot on messages.

Bruce: Hey, did you know X is out?

Rebecca: OMG, Bruce! When did it happen?

Bruce: Yesterday, and Y is next!

Rebecca: Lovely!

Rebecca: Na, you think so?

Bruce: Yep, times up!

Rebecca: Why?

Just like the conversation above, we had several conversations each day. We just couldn't get enough of each other's thoughts. We enjoyed discussing office politics. We also talked about our office colleagues and their behaviours as if we were two psychiatrists thoroughly discussing a case study. We also talked about what will happen in the next few days in the office and whether we were estimating all the events taking place in the office accurately. Our discussions were so long they could be compiled into ten novels. Here's another one of our interesting chats.

Bruce: *This office is a mess.*

Rebecca: *Why are you here, Bruce? You seem to have vast knowledge.*

Bruce: *I am kind of semi-retired.*

Rebecca: *Why?*

Bruce: *Again, why? (Don't ask me, her 'Why' will kill me one day, I still answered her.) I don't need anything anymore in life.*

Rebecca: *WHY Bruce?*

Bruce: *Why do you have so many whys??*

Slowly, our chats turned to topics about people and life at large. We spoke about anything and everything. We learned about each other's interests and daily haunts. We learned our general likes and dislikes. We learned how we thought about everything and our general perspectives of life.

Then our talks turned to our personal lives. Our frankness took me by surprise. I had never opened up to anyone in the last seven years. Yet, here I was with Rebecca pulling open my life like it was a book.

We used to chat daily. Before meeting Rebecca, I never felt like speaking to anyone. I spent the last seven years all alone, keeping everything I felt inside me. I came across so many people over the years, but no one really knew me in the previous years because I never felt like talking to anyone. With Rebecca, everything was different. I told her everything there was to know about me. She knew about my career, marriage, family, son, problems, divorce, and every single thing that I always felt like hiding away from the world. I could never understand what was so special about her that let me open up to her about everything.

There came a time I became habitual of messaging her and talking to her endlessly about anything and everything.

"She was like a subject to me as I like to read people and their behaviours. But when did the subject become the only subject? I really don't know."

The way she used to listen to me intently and with full attention and ask questions at the right time, it felt as if she could really visualise the scenario I was talking about. The comments, views and ideas she shared always felt as if they were coming from a place of vast experience in life. Our talks and the details we shared about each other's personal lives made me know the kind of person she was. I also understood the things she had gone through in her life and in her family till now. I don't know why, but I felt as if I had always known her and I felt confident enough to accept anything that would follow her. I don't know what made me so confident to face the consequences of the direction I was heading to. And then our chats became less each day.

I did not realise when I began missing our chats. Even if there was a gap of a few hours between our chats, it felt too long. We did message each other by default on a daily basis, though. This went on for many days. I kept reminiscing about the past and who she was, and how her nature used to be. I still remember she told me she used to live with her parents and sister back home before she moved to my city. She was also an educated woman and had huge respect for education. She was old school in her ways, too, just like I was. Old school people like us have a habit of mentioning our qualifications after our names while introducing ourselves to other people in a manner of pride and respect for our education. Rebecca had the same habit. Youngsters these days don't care about qualifications or education. No one was bothered about education these days. Anyone could enter any profession without respect to their qualification. Rebecca had the touch of the old school, where respect, honour and discipline mattered.

Rebecca: *How was the day, Bruce?*

Bruce: *God, how was yours?*

Rebecca: *Okay, kinda the same in the office. It's a mess.*

Bruce: *Yeah.*

Rebecca: *We talk a lot, and these things are not getting over by themselves.*

Bruce: *Yes.*

Rebecca: *I didn't realise it.*

Bruce: *Actually, I like talking to you, sharing talks...hmm, I like you. I mean, just mentioning it's just my feelings. A random feeling, hmm... I love you.*

Rebecca: *Hmm*

There, I let it slip one afternoon without giving it much thought. I was relaxing at my usual time with whisky and something to eat while we spoke over messages. It happened suddenly, and I let it slip. During the conversation, she just realised that we talked a lot, and I realised how I truly felt about her, and I told her so. I also told her it was just my feelings and I expected nothing in return. My heart was beating heavily, and I was scolding myself in my head. I was speaking to myself:

Bruce: *Bruce?~@# What the f*k did you just say? You're not supposed to say that! Shit! You're not entitled to do or think or talk this way.*

Bruce: *Come on Bruce, you're not supposed to enter into a relationship!*

Luckily, Rebecca was smart and mature. She didn't acknowledge or react to what I had just said to her and mentioned that there was something she had to take care of. She said it was late and that we would talk later and disappeared from the messages. After she was gone, I just jumped into my blanket and covered myself. I couldn't stop thinking of what I had just done. But I also felt relieved in a way. At least, now she knew how I felt about her.

A few days later, in the afternoon at work, I suddenly received a message from her.

Rebecca: *I want to meet you.*

Bruce: *With the HR??(I thought I was F*ed)*

Rebecca: *Seriously, I want to meet. Don't you want to?*

Bruce: *Of course.*

Until we managed to schedule a day and time to meet, I felt really uneasy. My stomach stayed upset for the next few days till the day we met in a restaurant. I meant I was feeling butterflies in my stomach. I told her so as well when we were messaging late at night before we could plan a meet.

Rebecca: *You ok?*

Bruce: *Yes, just have an upset stomach.*

Rebecca: *How?*

Bruce: *Because of the meeting appointment.*

Rebecca: *Mine too.*

Bruce: *Of course.*

I couldn't believe she was feeling the same way as I was. I was feeling different. It was after 7 years that I was up for going out. I didn't know what to wear, where to go, how to act, what to give her for a present, what cuisine to pick...etc. **I did know NOTHING!**

And then the day came when we met off work. She came in, and all I could say was, hi.

Bruce: *Hi.*

Rebecca: *Hi Bruce, early as usual?*

Bruce: *Yep.*

(She didn't know I was an hour and a half early at the restaurant we were supposed to meet at to check how it was. What were its surroundings like, and what was the path to it? I also wanted to check what was on the menu. And I wanted to check the location, the seating etc., like I was a spy who had come to do a recon of the entire location before a strike).

She looked pretty and decent. I wanted to compliment her, but I didn't.

The waiter got us the drinks we had ordered and also brought the flowers that I had instructed to get us when we ordered our first drinks. She admired the flowers, and we both smiled. At the moment, I had no worries about the outcome of our meeting. I knew how my life had been all those years, and I knew it was not possible for us to be together, but I felt really excited about spending time with her.

During our meeting, she tried to explain to me that it was not possible for us to go ahead in this relationship, and I understood, but she did not feel satisfied that I had understood her. We spoke on and off about different topics and about the office. We had a great time at the meeting, but even by the end of it, she didn't feel satisfied that I was alright with us not moving forward in this relationship. She did not feel convinced. At the end of our meeting, we bid goodbye and thanked each other for the time. A few days passed. We continued to stay in touch with each other via usual messages and chats about the office.

I took an off one day, and I was still in my pyjamas when I decided to start a chat with her in our usual messages. I don't know why, but I wanted to talk to her, even when it was via messages. I couldn't stay for long without talking to her. It just felt too difficult not to miss her. I couldn't help it.

Rebecca: *What's the plan?*

Bruce: *Nothing, just another normal day.*

Rebecca: *Wanna meet?*

Bruce: *Sure. (Oh GOD, damn sure!)*

Rebecca: *Place?*

Bruce: *Anywhere. (Hell, anywhere!)*

I didn't care which place she chose to meet, the only thing that mattered was we met. I was so excited I nearly jumped up out of my bed. She mentioned a place, and I agreed immediately. I didn't care where or how far it was located. I would make it to that place anyhow.

Honestly, I didn't know the place she had mentioned, but it didn't bother me at all. I could take a car, bus, train, aeroplane, or cycle, whatever it took to reach that place. I could get myself a couple of wings and fly over to that place on my own if that's what it took to get there. But I was going to find a way! Finally, the day of the meeting came, and we met. Rebecca had selected a beautiful park. We met and walked. Our long walk was interrupted by heavy rain. Rebecca was annoyed by the heavy downpour and the droplets on her glasses. The raindrops were falling on her face and down over her nose. To find some shade from the heavy downpour, we ran to the country pub. We ordered some domestic wine and talked a lot more than we had expected. I always enjoyed our talks and the explanations that Rebecca had. We noticed that both of us were feeling as if our talks were just not enough. They kept feeling as if they were incomplete. We didn't want to stop and leave. We felt if we left our talks halfway, we would never have the time to complete them again. So, we decided to meet again, and this time around, we chose the same park and the pub. In our next meeting, our talks were not focused on general life or practical life. Instead of that, our talks were more casual and what things we liked and disliked. For lunch, we ordered soup and some assorted snacks. After this meeting, we met once again the next week. This time, we chose the riverside. The calmness of water all around us made our day wonderful. We took to our day out early in the morning so we could enjoy the river and then breakfast and the rest of the festivities. We loved walking about the riverside. In this meeting, we talked about serious life and chatted about several things that were coming into our minds.

I didn't know what Rebecca was thinking of, but for me, my days were going by quite beautifully. In a span of a few days, we met several times. We spoke about several things like the office. Our topics were quite blended these days. We both realised that we enjoyed and felt really relaxed after meeting for a few hours a day. Not only that, but we also enjoyed meeting at the same place, usually a restaurant. To add flare to our meetings, we started meeting in different cuisine restaurants. We explored Thai, Vietnamese, Japanese, and English cuisines. Every week, I prayed that our days off were scheduled with each other so we could meet for the outing. I used to reason with God so we could meet.

Bruce: *God, I think that's okay to ask you if she can meet me some days.*

She had more faith in me than I had in myself. She didn't know the reason for my motivation to meet her regularly. I had recently gotten one motivation to meet her (her), but I didn't know if this was a permanent reason. But I believed good things happened for a good reason. Perhaps, I could not handle the good things in my life. Maybe I wasn't capable enough, or I was just scared.

Na... I think I would have over-cared.

Learn your place in someone's life so you don't overplay your part.

I loved listening to the explanations Rebecca gave as if I was a small kid and she was a teacher. She was so mature and yet so innocent. I could barely believe someone could bring this kind of affection out of me. At times, I felt as if she was irritated with my answers or remarks. To me, when she was criticising me, it looked as if she was scolding a child. I also loved how she dressed. Every single thing about her attire spoke of her beauty and the beauty of her nature. For instance, her sweater was just like her nature, warm and caring. In modern times, many girls avoided wearing sweaters, but Rebecca did, and it also suited her. It gave her an innocent traditional country touch that reflected her family's calm nature. When she was around me, it felt like I could smell nature's freshness around me or like I had glowing perfumed candles around me. Some of her expressions made me smile. I really enjoyed her 'rolling eyes expression', which made me a bit confused. She also had a habit of putting both her hands together when she was explaining something to me, just like Italians did. Everything about her, her talks, looks, and her pretty smile, were all so heart-warming for me.

My life wasn't as full of people and love as that of others, and that was one thing that had always weighed on me. I didn't have anything in life, and I didn't want anything, and I always felt as if something was missing. Rebecca filled the gap in my heart by just being there in my life. This was the reason that even when she left me for a little bit of time, I felt completely stranded. Her presence in my life had become pertinent. I didn't know why it was like this, but meeting her regularly became a special occasion for me. It brought me joy and satisfaction I cannot explain. This feeling made my happiness dependent on meeting Rebecca regularly. When she left for the holidays, I missed her more than I could explain. I also missed her on her off days when I couldn't see her in the office.

My separation from Rebecca, even temporarily, made me miss her so much that I decided to write a book. Maybe the book will keep her memories alive or keep me alive even when we couldn't be together. I already knew we were not going to be together for a long time, so I needed something to survive. She became a part of my daily routine. When Rebecca left, she went to visit her parents. I connected back with her the moment she got back home.

Bruce: *How were the holidays?*

Rebecca: *Lovely, feel really relaxed. And you? How are you feeling?*

Bruce: *I am ok (How could I tell her I was missing her like crazy?).*

Rebecca: *Sure?*

Bruce: *Yep.*

Bruce: *Ate Mama's food?*

Rebecca: *Lots.*

Bruce: *Must be chubby!*

Rebecca: *What? You mean fat?*

Bruce: *Hmm, I mean chubby! (Hell, oops, what did I say?)*

Chubby means like a doll (Pheeew...).

Rebecca: *HMMM.*

Bruce: *You look good, though, chubby and dolly.*

Rebecca: *Hmmm.*

Perhaps, I should have been more careful while choosing my words. Rebecca was obviously feeling overwhelmed after visiting her parents. Parents are the strength and the energy for their children. With them around, you are focused on your life, and you know what's wrong and what's right. She had just come back from home. She must be feeling content. In spite of being in a job here and a family back home, she was happy. She was sailing in two boats and was such a gentle lady. I didn't know what she thought about me or if it was normal for her to live her life after we parted ways.

A long time ago, I asked her:

Bruce: *You look upset! Have you had a fight with anyone?*

Rebecca: *No, I am fine.*

Rebecca was not upset due to any disagreement. She was upset because she was stressed about us. I believe that we get pulled towards things when we're stressed. Perhaps, she was feeling the same way, perhaps, I felt that too. But when she realised the direction she was heading into, she came back to life and became the practical person she was, and she made sure she brought me back to earth as well.

We knew that our relationship could not go any further from where it was at the moment. Yes, there was the factor of the age gap, but there was more of it... it was our separate realities... The way we lived our lives and our individual lifestyles were so different we couldn't jive with each other, maybe, we were just never meant to be (I don't know). She was so mature that she could understand how a person's lifecycle was. She understood everything, whether it was about a person, a partner, children, a job, savings, a future or any other simple thing that a person can dream of. I knew all of that too, but Rebecca was too stressed to explain that to me. I knew very well about all of this.

I also knew where I stood in life. I had no proper job, no future, no savings, no excitement, no ideas for family planning and many other simple things, not yet, at least. I could plan for all this but was not at the present time. I also felt it was not wise for someone to gamble in life, and pursuing Rebecca meant that I could be gambling on my and Rebecca's futures. I felt chasing after Rebecca would challenge both of our stability.

Rebecca: *You ok?*

Bruce: *Yep, as usual.*

Rebecca: *It cannot go further.*

Bruce: *I know.*

Rebecca: *I was scared you would be hurt.*

Bruce: *Na, I will be fine. I am not going to act crazy or kill myself. I will be fine. Well, I am still human, so I will be sad now and again... that's it.*

Rebecca: *No, I don't want you to be sad.*

Bruce: *One does not get everything in life.*

I learned from my experience with Rebecca that one could not make everyone happy in this world. I sat one night thinking of how stressed she was because of me. I could see it in her eyes. The person I cared for was stressed out because of me. I sometimes felt guilty for expressing my feelings to Rebecca. I had tried for the entirety of these 7 years not to hurt anyone more. But here I was again, hurting the person who I liked the most. Not intentionally, of course, but I had done the damage.

We could not stay together, but at least one of us could be happy and enjoy the beauty of nature and life. I know what pain is. As I have said earlier, I lived working for money, status, and pride, and I had many connections and friends. I was a wise guy, a made man (like in those gangster movies). I didn't play with money. I played with status. I had a row house, a garden, and a car, and I was known across the city, as I mentioned earlier. **Well, that story is for another day.**

Now, after 7 years, I was a changed man. I couldn't bear the thought of hurting anyone, and here the person in question was Rebecca, someone I loved and respected dearly. I decided to make her life a little less stressful. I reduced unwanted messages. I reduced sharing my feelings and expressions so she could feel normal. Over these years, I have become an expert in making people feel happy. I had done this for my parents and relatives. I showed them that I was fine. I could do the same for Rebecca. The book I wrote to preserve her memories had a front cover that clearly indicated Rebecca's place in my life, but I changed that front cover so it does not remind either of us of the time we spent, and I don't want people to know or trouble her.

I want her to be happy.

That's the best I can do, but for my own personal feelings, I need to be normal about this to myself. I did not try to alter this truth for myself at all. There was no point in it. **I simply cannot.**

I think I at least have the right to choose something for myself... let it be pain, what matters?!

"Life doesn't really give us choices, does it? We make do with what we are given. And sometimes even that is taken away. Life gives you all when you cannot handle it and takes it when you are ready to handle it. I still had power, the energy left to make things happen".

Often, when we think we have got it all sorted, life plays a trick on us. It takes away what we expect to stay in our lives. There might be no apparent meaning to it. Life doesn't care if you have worked hard for it or not. Life doesn't play fair. Life doesn't play by the rules you make. Life has its own way of doing things. Life is not a science experiment in controlled laboratory settings where you can study cause and effect. Life is so much more.

Sometimes, it comes to my thoughts that if we had met in a different situation, she would be a perfect simple partner for me. Well, I wouldn't have been that bad, either. We would have lived a simple life. We could have had a small family and enjoyed growing old together. I am a good cook, though!

I could feel the last few days of our meetings coming pretty fast, and I hoped for a last dinner so I could preserve her perfect memory forever. A dinner that might not happen. I was okay, as I said earlier. You don't get everything in life, sometimes, you get nothing too.

Anyways, I had only one thing left with me, and that was my book. And the only thing I was scared of was that even if a small part of this book would not be perfect, I was gonna lose my head. This book is the only thing that has the ability to control me and my feelings. This book means a lot to me. It gave me the strength to face our parting without any stress.

I want to tell you all... **"It takes a hell of a lot of pain to write reality".**

I requested one last date. I asked her to review the chapter about her in my book so she could see it and offer suggestions for changes and additions or deletions to it. I told her I wanted her to check it and let me know if I may have made some mistakes in some of the sentences. I won't be able to live with the guilt of conveying our story falsely. *(In reality, I just wanted to see her one last time and say our last goodbyes to each other in a satisfactory manner.)*

Bruce: *All ok?*

Rebecca: *Yes, tired.*

Bruce: *Up to you, if you can meet tomorrow? Just to finalise your chapter and this might be our last meeting, as you also have to plan and live your future. Cannot waste time on such things. I know it's stressful for you to bear with me, but this book is all I have, and it's just your chapter's main points that I need you to see. Then you can tell me my way.*

Rebecca: *Ok*

Rebecca was a very gentle lady, and she stressed about me too. She wanted me to forget everything and remain a good friend to her. She wanted me to understand that our relationship could not happen, we could only be good friends.

Bruce: *I agree with all that you said. What do you want me to do? You want me to keep smiling, I will. You want me to laugh, play, or enjoy movies, all these things I will do in my life. I can do* *anything for you. But my feelings are totally mine. I will not give that up at any cost. That's my identity. (I could feel my eyes getting wet as I wrote that in the message.)*

"You go out of my mind. It will never happen. I take you out of my mind. I will never let it happen".

My feelings for you will remain forever with me. "One gets stressed either thinking this might happen or that". In my case, I will remain the same, and so will my feelings. So, there is no point in being stressed.

Rebecca: *But Bruce, I cannot see you hurt!*

Bruce: *Rebecca, it's not in your hands, and neither is it in mine. So, let it go as it is my life. Trust me. I will be your best friend forever.*

We had our last dinner together. It was a quiet one. Maybe because we already knew it from the beginning, or we thanked God for at least the moments we had in our life. But I couldn't look into her eyes the entire dinner. I was scared of tears flowing out of my eyes and falling all over me, begging for one chance from her. I wanted to tell her in confidence that, 'Baby, I can do it. I can do everything for you. Please give our relationship a chance'. But I knew I had to control my emotions. That was what was good for us. We thanked each other for dinner, hugged and said goodbye to each other.

The moment I felt her leaving, everything just stopped around me. I could only feel the cold breeze on my face. I could see her catching the bus, and the bus drove far, far and far away till it faded. It was as if it had sunk into the ocean. I could see just an empty road. Everything was still like time had just frozen until a drop rolled down my cheeks, and I realised I was standing in the middle of the road all alone. It was a single drop of tear. Maybe the rest had dried up.

I wished God to be with her and protect and help her whenever she felt low.

I reached home early in the morning. I felt empty but not tired. Once again, I wanted to sleep. But this time, I was really tired and sleepy. I got into my pyjamas and headed to my bed. My mind was just wondering **whether she would ever come back or even visit me at least once in my life. I was just praying that we could still be in touch via messages**. I fell asleep.

Rebecca had not just left my life, she had also parted ways with the company we worked for. In a few days, I, too, left the company. I couldn't bear the essence of her aroma in the air. I could not just stare at the door of my office every day and pray that she walked in at least once. Every day I was at the company, I kept feeling as if someone was squeezing and holding my stomach. Every day was the same, and every time every day was a sad disappointment even after I knew she had gone long ago. I used to come to work early just to feel like she was still around in the office. Even when the office was crowded, I felt alone. The atmosphere was too heavy for me, and I felt tired every day. Ever since Rebecca left, I started imagining her at every same place I used to see her at once. At every corner or every road we walked on, I could see her clearly. At every candle shop, and sweater shop, I kept thinking of her. Everything reminded me of her. **I could not even stand looking at her workstation. I could feel her vibes there.** Every message beep still gives me a jerk in my stomach because I think it's Rebecca texting me.

For the first time in my life, I wished that someone would be there to hold me on the last day of my work. I needed someone to listen to me and hold me. The communication between Rebecca and me changed from very frequent to barely any. From hundreds of messages in a day, we went to two or three messages in a day.

I got this message from her four days after she left.

Rebecca: *I think it's all my fault to drag you in and give you hope. I am sorry, Bruce, we cannot continue. I cannot give you what you want!*

Bruce: *Us to get married?*

Rebecca: *Yes.*

Bruce: *Ok, then, what about without marriage?*

Rebecca: *Still cannot. There are all other things that matter to me. I cannot avoid them. Even my parents won't agree.*

Bruce: *Did you speak to them?*

Rebecca: *No, but I know what they will say, and I will not ask them.*

I didn't know what was happening and going on in the world at that moment.

Rebecca: *I am feeling bad, and it's my fault to hurt you.*

Bruce: *It's ok. I'm fine.*

Rebecca: *Bruce, you've been a very nice person, you know that. You've been very kind and helpful when I needed someone around. Bruce, can I return the thing you gave me.*

Bruce: *No, keep it... but don't throw it. Thank you for the time we spent, and all the best for your career.*

Rebecca: *Thank you, and I am sorry.*

Bruce: *It's ok. Just remember, if you require any help/ assistance, I am around the corner.*

Rebecca: *Same here for you, Bruce.*

Bruce: *Goodnight.*

Rebecca: *Goodnight.*

My ears were hurting as I could not bear the sound of my heart beating so hard. My body was cold, and I just went to the bathroom and began crying. I couldn't breathe. My heart was paining as if it was getting an attack. I could feel the blood moving in the nerves of my whole body as if the nerves were going to explode.

My mind was constantly talking, or was it me murmuring softly? I think I was speaking to God. I could hear it out loud as well.

Bruce: *God... I could have done it... happiness, family, career, money... etc., I can get it all... I can do it for her, I can do anything for her... She knows that very well... But the only factor was age... there was the age gap... for which I could do nothing. I studied and googled if there was anything I could do about the age factor. Was there any medicine or experiment going in any corner of the world? I read that Harvard was experimenting on rats but had not yet started on humans... but after doing my research, I knew I was looking for something that did not exist.*

The thing that hurt me the most was when she mentioned she wanted to give me my gift back. I felt as if she was trying to buy or compensate me for not reciprocating the feelings I had for her... I had given her a watch. And it was not just a watch, it had my feelings and the time we had spent together. That time was more precious than any diamond. It took me days to decide and set the budget to get that watch. It was the moments we had spent that were captured in time in the watch I had gifted her. My feelings for her were precious. They were purely mine and not something money could buy.

Those who have a 'why' to live can bear with almost any 'how'.

She had become my 'why'... but that 'why' was not for me...

"I always ask life... Can you be more messed up than this? Life replies... challenge accepted!"

I was still speaking to GOD. I cried my heart out, emptying everything I was feeling inside to my isolation and God. There was no one around to hear me whine and scream. I could at least let it all out. I didn't know what happened to make me lose it, but I did.

Bruce: *Why me, GOD? Many people say I am a good person! Really? Does this happen to good people? Or they were just lying. But how much more good do I have to become? Just tell me at least what I have to do for my sin or to become good or anything. I mean, just tell me, what should I do? I don't know what I am supposed to do... I was doing every good thing I could, but it's just driving me crazy because I am tired of doing everything, and then again, it's not enough.*

God, how long will I have to stay alone? It's been seven years. I have been trying to be good to people and to the world. I am tired, very tired. I have kept myself deprived of all worldly matters. I have been living simple, eating simple, and thinking simple. Just tell me how long or even tell me never. But tell me something!

"You can't cry when you're already empty."

After Rebecca, I was once again alone in my life. Again nothing was left in my life. Now I was a hundred per cent sure and was confident that I still have to pay for my sins. I have to pay for my sins while I was alive. More than death, my life would be full of suffering. That's why I did not die when I tried to take my life years back. Death is of less value for compensating for my sins. I have to suffer more. I have to live with it. So, I decided to live on and keep the pain alive inside me forever. It's now a part of my routine. Every day, I take out time for it... I sit and think over the piercing thoughts like knives and memories of the wounds of my past so that my wounds never heal, and I enjoy the sweet pain. I began doing this every evening before going to bed.

I wanted to tell her at the bus stop on our last day that if ever she wanted, she would find me as the same person when I was with her at the same place, forever. But I couldn't even do that as the moment she had left had frozen, except her leaving was in slow motion.

This was the second time when I just stared at life for taking my peace again. I couldn't say a word.

But I had memories, the sweet pain and this book to live with.

And I learned life is a journey.

I didn't realise when I fell asleep unconscious on the bed.

Good memories are the most precious gift anyone can give you.

The Peaceful Sunset

I am somewhere up there in the night sky full of stars, looking over you, smiling and wishing you good always!!

Maybe I was tired, and my body could not take all the pain, so I fell asleep almost as if I was unconscious. I didn't know when this pain of mine would end.

Life is a journey. All that you meet either gives you a lesson or a memory. If the memories are good, they hurt more. If they are bad, they turn into lessons. When I look behind in my life and see my loved ones progressing and happy in life, I feel I have lived the journey of my life beautifully.

"Beautiful memories hurt more."

Many of my friends and family members are still in touch with me. Whenever they give me a call, it feels great to hear their voices and how they are doing in life. And Rebecca... How can I forget her? Oh, yes! She calls me quite often. Her voice is the same, and I can visualise her smile still, even after so many years.

It had now been 4 years since our last dinner. We are good friends now, and we respect each other. She called me a few weeks ago. She had recently delivered a baby princess and wanted to send me her photo with the kid. She and James had a wonderful family. Both had good jobs, and they were settled, but Rebecca had taken maternity leave for the time being.

James and Rebecca had gotten married two years ago. James was a very caring gentleman, and he kept her happy. What a great celebration it was! I saw the pictures she sent me. I had made peace with Rebecca leaving a long time ago, and I fully understood the reasons behind it. I also understood that life had to go on. Hers had grown by leaps and bounds.

Rebecca: Bruce! How are you? Drinking?

Bruce: Hey, my lady! I am good...Drinking...? Na... Just a little.

Rebecca: Are you sure?

(Ahh... her questions will never end!)

Rebecca: Sending you the kid's photo.

Bruce: Wow...please send it fast. Can't wait to see her. Is everything okay, the kid's health? Your health?

Rebecca: All are fine. Don't worry, Bruce!

Bruce: Dinner?

Rebecca: Had it already, soup (as she cannot miss her meals).

Bruce: Lovely!

(OMG, she looks exactly like her mom!)

Bruce: *Wow, such a beautiful princess. And what the heck did you let her wear?*

Rebecca: *Bruce, Language@#!*

Bruce: *Sorry, I mean, it's summer, and you got her to wear a sweater? Crazy!*

Rebecca: *It's snowing here in my country.*

Bruce: *Hahaha, yes, yes, I forgot. Anyways, rest all fine?*

Rebecca: *Yes, rest all fine. You ok?*

Bruce: *Yes, I am.*

Rebecca: *Are you sure?*

Bruce: *Hahaha, yes, yes, I am fine.*

Bruce: *Anyways, you both take care and take good care of the kid.*

Rebecca: *Thanks, Bruce. Sleep well.*

Bruce: *You too. Sleep tight.*

I have come a long way from where I started out. The incident that changed my life forever and then meeting Rebecca and losing her, which once again changed my life fully, all had their own purpose. I am grateful that the first incident and Rebecca both happened, and I could feel that these events had allowed me to live with nature and with life rather than chasing behind worldly things.

I have learned how beautiful life is... and so amazing!

Often, it is the small things that we overlook. I think that is what life is trying to teach us. That little things matter. That we have to be grateful for them. We have to notice them. And sometimes, we notice them only when the big things are taken away from us.

For the first time in my life, I actually began believing that there was an alternative perspective to this. That perhaps it was not my fault, the things that I have been through. I have started looking at it from an outsider's perspective. From that outlook, I was able to forgive myself for the things I had done and forgive others who had done things to me. But I could never let the grief go. On days when my grief and my guilt became unbearable, I allowed myself a good cry, but that too only for ten minutes a day in the bathroom. Then my crying for the day is done, and I don't look back.

I had decided that what was important was my wellbeing. I would fight. I would not let my thoughts take over, but to be honest, it was Rebecca's memories and this book that kept me going until now. Today, I can safely say that I have survived the onslaught of destiny, maybe not so cheerily, but I have managed to live through it. Now, my life is all about my son and how I can enjoy it to the fullest with him. My son is coming next month for vacation. I love to see him. We might travel to see CK and his family. It's been a long time since I retired.

I have managed to live life all these years imaging my parents, brother and family, my son, CK and his family and Rebecca as being one very big family. I could see them all happy even when I closed my eyes. ***Yes, Rebecca was a part of my life, too, at least in my emotions.***

I sometimes sit and think about the mistakes I have made in my life and what I would have done differently. You know what? There is not a single thing I would do differently. I believe that each of our mistakes makes us stronger. They are our life lessons. They make us grow. And I think that is the most important thing in life. To keep making mistakes and learning from them so that we never stop growing.

So here's to mistakes, and here's to life itself!

Our lives are what we make of them. And we must own them whether we have a very successful life or we have difficulties, it doesn't matter. All that matters is that life brings with it experiences that teach us something new.

We often see some things as too big or too little based on the circumstances we are going through. In the same manner, our defeats are magnified in our own heads because we focus on what we have lost rather than on what we actually have.

I would grab life, and I would live it.

To make life more meaningful, we need to create a treasure trove of memories that will keep us strong. We need to find our own little comfort zones. More than anything, we need to find beauty even where there is none. It exists. Always. We just need to know where.

Our mind is our biggest enemy. But it can also be our biggest friend. There's so much beauty in life. We only have to look!

It has now been 10 years since Rebecca and I had our last dinner, but here I am loving and kicking it.

Yes, I have lived my life, and I am happy for whatever happened.

No regrets, no pain, no grief.

Now, looking back, I cannot believe that once, all I wanted to do was take my life. Once upon a time, I was so lost that I was too drunk to realise that I had taken pills to kill myself. Suicide was not something I had ever thought I could plan. Today, I don't know how I managed to get over the first blow of my life, the incident that changed everything. Sometimes, I feel it was good that I had encountered death, otherwise, I wouldn't know the other half of real life, and I also probably wouldn't have met **HER.**

Now I feel grateful for everything that happened in life, and I wish that I could tell my story to the world.

Well, I am a bit tired for now after an evening walk and completing this book. I will share with you my story of how I had lived in status for years and what happened seven years ago. Now, life had turned fairly normal, and my regular routine was back. I have just had a double shot of whiskey and some soup and retired to my bed. It's 7 pm already, and the sun has set to a dark night. I could see the stars shining in the sky through my window. I see them every night, smile, wish her goodnight and fall asleep.

I could hear my phone beeping in the far distance. I was woken up by my alarm.

The peaceful sunset was a dream.

When I had slept, my world had ended after the goodbye forever message from Rebecca. I sat up and realised that it was only last week when Rebecca and I had our last dinner. I realised Rebecca won't be there anymore. I will not see her again, but I did not feel sad inside. I think I couldn't feel anything. I felt like I wouldn't miss her absence anymore. Perhaps, it was her destiny to move on in life, get married, and have a wonderful family and a lovely daughter. Maybe everything I saw in my dream was going to come true eventually. She had to live her life.

My reminder rang, and it read, 'Busy day today'.

It's busy at work today with some kind of event scheduled during the day. I got dressed and had some breakfast.

I took my bag, stepped outside and locked my door behind me as I left for work.

I saw the shining blue sky outside, the roads were wet. It looked as if it had rained. It was crowded on the roads as this was the peak office hour of the day. **I was still thinking if I would ever see her again.** As I walked into the crowd, I was thinking about everything and observing other people doing more or less the same. Perhaps, each of the people on the streets had something on their minds as well. Maybe they had their own sorrows, grief and happiness to ponder over. Perhaps, they had their own struggles to deal with. I didn't know, but I did know about my troubles, and I never let my grief dampen. It stayed afresh in my memories. My grief was like an open wound that just wasn't healing. I never even wanted to heal it.

The Answer to pain is pain itself.

But life goes on.....

Two years later...

Jack: Hey, Bruce, coming for drinks tonight?

Bruce: Great, but have to be back home before ten.

Jack: No way. Why?

Bruce: Have some work.

Although I had found a new friend at work and Jack's presence had improved my social life a lot, but I still couldn't let go of the grief I was feeling. I had a habit of having drinks in the evening and thinking about everything that had happened in my life. How could I explain to him that my evenings were dedicated to sitting with myself and grieving for years to come?

The wounds that I love...

But I still pray every day for her.

God will watch over her for her wellbeing. As I have asked him to do so.

Receiving As It Comes

Life is not a having and a getting, but a being and a becoming.

Life comes with all of its colours and flavours. Sometimes, it's rainbows and butterflies, at other times, it's full of rainy days. However, the one thing that is constant about life is that it changes constantly. With every new change in life, whether happy or sad, we learn to grow. My life has been an ordeal that has broken me down into several tiny pieces almost twice. And yet, there's not a thing I would change about it. I have learned to accept my life the way it is. Better yet, I have accepted everything that has happened to me as it is. I firmly believe, all the experiences I have been through in life, were meant to happen and each has taught me something valuable in life.

Among everything else, I have accepted the following important things that I feel everyone should accept in life in order to move on from the trauma and pain they have been through[1].

1. Your Own Self

The first thing you MUST accept about you, is **YOUR OWN SELF**. Your personality, the way you are, the way you have been shaped by the circumstances you have endured in life, you have to accept yourself as a whole.

2. **You Will Only Get Older**

The next most important point of acceptance for you is that of your age. You will not be getting any younger as the years go by. The harsh reality of life is that you will never have the chance to experience something again and that too differently. An unfortunate experience will remain as it is no matter how many years get between that experience and you. Just accept it.

3. **You Will Always Lose People**

It doesn't matter how powerful you are as a person, you will always lose people. Either they will part ways with you because their life comes to an end or they find their life path to be separate from yours and walk away from you themselves. In any case, you can never keep someone by your side forever. While someone is still a part of your life, love them and show them that you love them. Don't hold back from expressing your feelings towards them.

4. **There Is No Way To Control Other People**

Accept that others you know are different from you. People have diverse traits and that's what makes them their own unique selves. If you try to make others similar to you, it destroys their own individuality. We often do this with the people that are close to us such as our family members, our spouses or our siblings or children. But we need to learn that people may sometimes hate us, at other times disagree with us majorly but in any case, they will always be different from us and that is why, there is diversity in the world and we must respect this diversity.

---

[1] Declutter The Mind. (2022). Acceptance of What Is: 17 Things to Accept in Life. Blog. https://declutterthemind.com/blog/acceptance/

5. It May Not Be Possible For You To Experience Everything

Life is full of several different experiences. Some are great, while others not so much. You wish to live some experiences while there are times when you avoid certain things. Often you look at others and think, only if you had the opportunity to experience what they were living but you must know that you may never have the chance to experience a few things in life. The sooner you accept this, the easier it gets for you in the long run. You can desire many things in life but they won't always come to pass and you will have to stay content with what you get.

After learning about acceptance, I have come to realise that everything gets easier when you finally accept these things and it paves the way for you to move forward with comfort.

With acceptance, comes healing from the pain of the bad thing that happened to you in life. One negative event disorients you and makes you feel like you have lost yourself or a big part of your personality. You feel disappointed and disillusioned. An overwhelming feeling of instability appears in your life. When you feel unstable by the events that happened to you, that you had no control over, that begin to define who you are as a person, you tend to lose your composure.

In such a case, you MUST learn to cope with the change that has taken place in your life. This change may be too difficult to handle, it may be hard to swallow or tough to stay steady with, it may have a severe effect on your health, your job, or even your personality. Though none of this should matter. Instead your ability to deal with such a change matters. You should put all of your efforts into dealing with the change you have experienced rather than letting it put you down. In order to stay focused and not lose sight of what needs to be done, you must follow the RACE model. It comprises of the following 4 simple steps[2]:

1) Resist your resistance to change.

2) Accept that which is not possible for you to change.

3) Choose what you want to change, that way, you are able to reclaim your own power to change.

4) Embrace the change that has taken place in your life by staying open to change in the future as well.

The next thing I learned when I looked deeper into acceptance is the concept of radical acceptance. Simply defined, radical acceptance is the acceptance of something happening to you, without judging it. In this way, you do not feel the negative effects of the experience as hard as you get hit by it. With radical acceptance, you learn to detach yourself from all the bad things you have experienced and let it become a solid part of who you are, without it hurting you[3].

---

[2] Rackliffe, C. (2022). Coping with Change: 4 Ways to Survive Any Major Life Event. https://www.crackliffe.com/words/2020/7/20/coping-with-change-4-ways-to-survive-any-major-life-event

[3] Cuncic, A. (2022). What Is Radical Acceptance?. Emotions. VeryWellMind. https://www.verywellmind.com/what-is-radical-acceptance-5120614

When there is a deep pain attached to a certain situation or an event, it gets tough to let it go because it is not easy to move on from. Through radical acceptance, your healing journey can begin and you can start to learn to detach yourself from the things you cannot control and that are out of your power of influence. Radical acceptance states that one must see a negative event with compassion and forgiveness for yourself. By forgiving yourself, you can move on from the negative event and its effects and allow yourself the peace you deserve[4].

After years of suffering through the pain of what I have had to deal with in life, losing everything important to me twice and dealing with an unstable emotion, I have finally begun to make peace with everything that happened. I have started receiving life as it comes to me rather than expecting it to be something that it's not. I have now clearly understood that life will never be as per my expectations. It will always be full of curve balls and I will have to learn how to tackle these curve balls and navigate these with grace.

---

[4] Richards, J. (2022). The Healing Power of Radical Acceptance: Help Yourself to Accept What Is. Michelle Maidenberg. https://michellemaidenberg.com/the-healing-power-of-radical-acceptance-help-yourself-to-accept-what-is/

Forgiveness is the best form of love. It takes a strong person to say sorry and an even stronger person to forgive.

Forgiving

We win by tenderness. We conquer by forgiveness.

Pain was the constant I had learned to live with for a very long time. There were times when I felt as if I was gliding through a dark tunnel and there was never going to be any light in my life. I couldn't find my way out of this very dark and twisted tunnel that seemed never-ending and full of pain and misery. Pain used to be such a constant in my life, it had become similar to breathing to me. Until someone else became a constant...

Rebecca's presence in my life made it better than I had expected. I learned to live through the pain because she stood by me. And then I lost her too and the pain came back for the second time. I lost everything all over again and found new reasons to be angry with myself and not let go of the pain I was previously in.

At this juncture of my life, while trying to climb my way out of my misery, I learned the value of forgiveness. There were many things that had gone wrong in my life only due to the decisions that I had taken. I had decided to get close to Rebecca. It was my decision to become so close to her and when she left because she had to, I couldn't blame anyone but myself. She was younger and had a bright prospect for a life before her. I was never going to be her first choice for a partner in life and I had made peace with that reality even when her thought came to my mind. I just feel a great sense of gratitude when I think about having her in my life as a friend. Her personality is one that adds value to my life, knowing that she is happy and content where she is in life, makes me happy too.

Through this experience and my previous experience when the incident happened, I learned the value of forgiving myself. Forgiveness for your own self may seem like an easy idea but it is actually one of the more difficult aspects of life.

Self-forgiveness has nothing to do with losing accountability for yourself or dropping responsibility for the things you have done in life. You do not lose sight of what you have done or take it lightly or make it a matter of 'it doesn't matter what I've done', in fact, it takes a lot more of your effort to forgive yourself than to forgive another person. When forgiving yourself, you must do the following[5]:

- Take care of your emotions

- Take responsibility for the wrong that was done by you

- Stay kind and compassionate to yourself

- Feel remorse for your actions

- Apologise to yourself and begin to make amends for the wrongs you have done.

- Find out the ways in which you can make the negative experience a learning one for yourself.

- Try to make better choices in the future.

---

[5] Cherry, K. (2023). How to Forgive Yourself. Happiness. Very Well Mind. https://www.verywellmind.com/how-to-forgive-yourself-4583819

Basically, self-forgiveness focuses on the following 4 R's that will help you, for starters, forgive yourself so you can move on to forgiving others and grow out of the negative situation you have been through.

1) Responsibility

2) Remorse

3) Restoration

4) Renewal

I have found that I have had the chance to experience all four of the R's and it is through them that I have had the courage to forgive myself. Once I managed to forgive the mistakes I made, I found it easier to forgive others who had hurt me. Yet, I took my sweet time because it was still a very hard thing to do for me. Time taught me that forgiving others was not something that was meant to make life easy for them, it was the thing that would make life easy for me.

The emotional wounds I had received in my life needed to heal and I learned that forgiveness of the people who had hurt me would help me heal.

Some people who us a lot of harm, either by abandoning us or by hurting us in a manner that is irreparable. Forgiving such people may seem impossible and unjust but the advantages of forgiving people like that are a lot more than the pain you carry when you keep a grudge against that because it keeps reminding you of the bad they have done and it keeps hurting you.

As per popular research, forgiving someone had three major indications. The first is that you don't feel upset or angry when you think about what happened to you. The second is that you do not feel resentful towards the person who hurt you. And the third is when you really feel like doing something good for the person who you have forgiven[6].

I also learned that forgiving others has the following benefits:

1) You feel less anxious when you forgive

2) You do not feel depression

3) You feel empowered and hopeful

4) You don't hurt anyone else

---

[6] Laurence, E. (2023). Forgiveness: How to Forgive Yourself and Others. Forbes Health. https://www.forbes.com/health/mind/ways-to-forgive-yourself-and-others/#:~:text=%E2%80%9CSecond%2C%20forgiveness%20means%20not%20being,way%20of%20forgiveness%2C%20he%20continues.

Looking deeper into forgiveness, I was able to understand that forgiveness has nothing to do with what the other person has done to you. It has everything to do with your own self. You heal by forgiving the other person and keep your own self healthy and happy. By forgiving others, you overcome the emotions of anger, resentment, shame, fear and sadness. You are able to develop feelings of gratitude, compassion and love for yourself and for others[7].

My life-changing experiences also made me realise that forgiveness is important for moving forward in life. We all have an inner critic inside of us who keeps telling us what we have done wrong. It makes us feel guilty and reminds us of all the bad things we have done or could have done differently. Unfortunately, while this critic sometimes, helps us get better at understanding how we can improve, at times, it also holds us back from being who we are. While out inner self constantly criticises what we have been doing, we are unable to empathise with our own feelings and hurt ourselves, holding our own selves back from moving forward in life[8].

When you don't forgive, you constantly carry a physical and emotional toll that wears you down and makes it difficult for you to move forward in life because you feel heavy all the time. The only cure of this heaviness is to release the resentment and forgive, you feel light enough to move forward!

I have come a long way from the night of the incident when I woke up to realise I nearly killed myself. After that night, I never thought I would be able to grow out of the doom and gloom feelings I had been experiencing since my separation. I abandoned everything I cherished (things I will speak openly about in Part 1 of this book), and began living a simple life to cope with the pain I had been through. On my way to find some peace, I met someone I had never planned on making someone important to me, Rebecca. She became an important part of who I was at this juncture of my life. I learned to speak my mind with her again and I began cherishing life again with her presence. She helped me love and laugh once again and yet, upon her departure, I experienced the second traumatic blow of my life.

Once again, I struggled and learned to grow out of the pain I was in and once again, I managed to climb out of my misery. Here I am taking one step at a time, to the next important thing for me, living in a peaceful situation, taking life as it is, accepting of everything that is happening to me and forgiving myself and others who had wronged me. I am still learning and growing every single day and I believe this learning and moving forward will continue still on, till I meet the next challenge of my life and life teaches me how to overcome it and still be alive, healthy, happy and stay capable of making others happy.

---

[7] Good Therapy. (2018). It's For You, Not Them: Forgive to Help Yourself Heal. Blog. https://www.goodtherapy. org/blog/its-for-you-not-them-forgive-to-help-yourself-heal-0710184

[8] Cooks-Campbell, A. (2022). Stop Beating Yourself Up! Learn How to Forgive Yourself to Move Forward. BetterUp. https://www.betterup.com/blog/how-to-forgive-yourself